What are people saying about If There's a Chance

I LOVE this book, if you like to laugh then this is the book for you. If There's a Chance: Prank Rule # 3 touches on has a little bit of everything. Love, laughter, and family.

Melissa/Amazon

I love George and Kyle's relationship as brother and sister. I enjoyed every second of this book and explanation of rule three!

Andrea/Amazon

Reading about Kyle and her brothers' prank wars was hilarious. At different spots in the book I found myself laughing so hard I had tears running down my face.

Kimberly/Amazon

Seeing the inside of Kyle and George's closeness is endearing. From their fussing, pestering each other, pranks that lead to injury, and protecting one another even when it is not wanted, you see a deep love of siblings that most of us wish we had.

Regina/Goodreads

If There's a Chance

By Sidonia Rose

Amanda,

Little Sisters
Are Awesome!

Sidonia
Rose

Other books by Sidonia Rose

Love U ~ Series

Love Shots

Proof

Pierce Family Prank Rules ~

If There's a Chance

If There's a Chance

By Sidonia Rose

Copyright © 2014 Sidonia Rose

ISBN:978-1941560037 (MAZHook inc LLC)

If There's a Chance

Pierce Family Prank Rules

Sidonia Rose

Pierce Family Prank Rules

1. Stay out of Mom's bathroom.
2. No live rodents in the house.
3. If there is a chance of an ER visit, find something else.
4. If there is a mess, we are both responsible for clean-up.
5. The smoke alarms are tied to the security system and the fire department will show up

Dedicated to all of the heroes

that don't wear capes.

Thanks for everything you do.

Table of Contents

CHAPTER 1

Summer

4 Years Earlier

George

My sister is the biggest pain in my keister!

I can't even guess how many times I've said that in my lifetime. My summer plans as usual include a part time job, the extra cash helps. More importantly, I just want to relax and not have to worry about too much. I know that's going to be hard with my father traveling most of the summer, but that isn't really anything new. He travels for work all the time.

Mom likes to fuss over every little detail, but for the most part she lets us make our own choices. I get along well with both of my younger brothers; I even get along with our bratty kid sister. This summer might be the exception though. She has always been the over achiever in the family, I heard my parents say once she was just trying to keep up. My brother Dean has taken an internship at some company in Baltimore City and is going to stay with a friend there for most of the summer. True to form, my sister also needed to find a summer internship and has taken one that will run for six weeks. She did the same thing last year, so she has been bragging that she is a second year intern.

If There's a Chance

She starts today and I was nominated to drive her to and from her new job. A job she isn't even getting paid to do. She's also a morning person, so she hasn't shut-up since we got in the car. She alternates between singing along to the radio and telling me about this great opportunity she found.

"I can't believe I got picked for this. I mean, I heard they had over three hundred people apply for this program. I only had the one interview but isn't this exciting?" I can see her from the corner of my eye and she is bouncing in her seat right now. "It's pretty great that I get to spend so much time with you too. This will be the best thirty minutes every morning."

I don't offer anything other than a grunt in response. She knows I'm not much of a morning person. It might only be thirty minutes for her but I still have to get back home, so it's at least an hour for me. I watch my little sister apply a fresh coat of lip gloss to her lips. "Don't you have enough of that stuff on?" I open the window a little to let some fresh air in, "That stuff smells gross."

Dropping the lip gloss into her bag, "It's not going to work George. This is a great opportunity for me and I can't wait. I can meet new people, make new friends," She pauses before adding quieter, "It's a co-ed program, so that might work in my favor."

I laugh; there is no way she is bringing some guy home from this summer program of hers. "I thought this was going to look good on your college application? I didn't know this was a dating service."   .

She snorts at me, "I would have to date for a dating service to work. I just want to leave my options open. It will be kind of nice not having you boys hanging around scaring the guys away. Besides this is my second summer with them and they offer scholarships to second year interns."

I watch her change the radio station again until she finds another song she likes. I groan when I hear my sister sing along about kissing a girl. I swear tomorrow I need more coffee before I will get in the car with her again.

I drop her off and watch as she walks into the building. I have to give my sister credit, she never shies away from a challenge. I pulled up and she jumped out of the car and took herself right into the office building, no hesitation. I guess after being the little sister all these years nothing scares her.

After an entire week of driving Kyle to and from her internship she hasn't let up. She is still just as upbeat as her first day. Every day is non-stop chatter about her day and the people she is working with. The company she is working for has a large media division with everything from magazines to television stations. Their summer program is going to explore implementing social media into mainstream advertising. I guess the best way to do that is with high school students; after all they are the ones primarily using it.

I was out late last night and getting up extra early so she could pick up donuts was not part of my plans. The radio has remained off because the noise is just too much; of course that hasn't stopped her from talking.

"So, then Brad was telling Melody that he likes when I wear blue. Really, who even says that? I mean I wore blue once and it wasn't even like a good blue color. It was kind of that bland, faded blue."

I can't believe this is my morning, traffic and debating the color blue. "Stop, just stop talking. When we get there point out who this Brad person is and I will take care of it. He won't like you in any color."

"Oh, we are not doing that. You promised you would stay out of my life this summer." That's the sister I know and love; now she's good and mad.

I slam on the brakes again as everyone in front of me comes to stand still, "I am staying out of your life! I'm just going to help Brad with his for a few minutes. It will all work out."

3

"You can just leave him alone. Besides I heard his parents know the owner or something. He lives in Virginia and I wouldn't date him anyway." Her voice trails off before she adds; "Besides I wouldn't even know what to say to him, he always eats lunch with Ashley C. No one ever likes me anyway."

I guess maybe I do feel kind of bad for her. She's popular enough in school but there is no one that will ever date her. With three older brothers and Joey looking out for her; well they just won't mess around with her. I know she wants to change that but it's not happening any time soon. When the right guy comes along he won't care if she has over protective brothers and he will tell us to back off. So far that guy hasn't come along.

Her voice gets a little whiney, "Just promise you won't do anything to Brad."

The way she says his name makes me think he's one of those geeky guys from high school everyone picks on. "I won't embarrass you around your new friends."

I pull up to the front of the building and she grabs for her stuff, "I wasn't worried about that. It's not like you could really embarrass me. I think I got over that a long time ago."

She slams the door and it's like she threw down the gauntlet this morning. I haven't pranked her since I got home from school and she is due for something big. I will have to think about this today.

CHAPTER 2

George

One drive home, three phone calls, a borrowed costume, a talk with security, and I'm sitting outside of Kyle's internship office. She said I can't embarrass her, well I happen to think she's wrong. The best part is I have plenty of help. It didn't take much to convince my brother Sean to help me today. He's going to take photos and most likely some video clips. I'm going to make sure we get videos uploaded for everyone to see. I still have to be able to reign in her temper though, when she's mad look out. I swear she has a full Irish temper that no one wants to mess with. So I called Joey, he's always been a friend and he's usually referred to as Kyle's fourth brother.

I had to call a few guys I know from high school to look for the ape costume. I knew someone would have this old costume we used our senior year. When I got to the office I pitched the idea to the guy at the security desk and he about laughed himself off his chair. He thought it was the funniest thing he ever heard. I just told him I needed to teach my little sister a lesson and the best way to do it is to embarrass her.

I know she has lunch soon and luckily they let me use an empty office to dress in this costume. I slide on the large hands before I enter the lobby. I watch as a group of ladies, all wearing smart business suits, look at me like I just landed space ship. I made a sign to hold today and I flash it so they can read it. They all start laughing and pointing at me. I smile to myself and wave to them.

The sign simply says,

Do you Know

Kyle Pierce?

I'm her Brother

The sign was Sean's idea and kind of last minute. We were already on our way here when we talked about it. So we stopped and bought the supplies to make the sign. I wish we would have thought to put her picture on the sign but if we had no one would remember her name. This way they will all remember her name. I thought fliers would be better but we couldn't get them printed until this afternoon.

Some people might say this is a bit mean but she will get over it. At least our parents won't hear about it before it's over. The last prank we pulled didn't go over so well at home. Dad went over the top and started giving us rules to follow; it really takes the fun out of doing this. Luckily there is no stopping me today.

I see Sean in the lobby and wave to him. He picks up his camera and starts recording me. I bounce back and forth from foot to foot, then start running to the camera. When I'm close enough I brace myself and let the fur on my feet slide me across the lobby.

I bounce around and get warmed up for a long afternoon. It's a bit hard to see and hear everything; so both Sean and Joey are talking loud for me. I see the guys at the security desk laughing and one of them is taking our picture.

More people are stopping to look. I wave to them and point to my sign. Sean keeps right on recording. I expect Kyle's temper to go nuclear on this, which is Joey's job. He can intercept Kyle and keep her from getting herself fired. We joke that Joey is like her fourth brother but I'm pretty sure he has liked her for years.

I see some of the interns leaving for lunch. A few of them must know Kyle because they stop and start asking questions. It's a little hard to hear them with the costume on and the noise level is increasing in the lobby. I wave at Sean and point to the doors, I want him to know I'm moving. It's time to take this outside.

I go out and find a nice spot in the shade. It's hot today but not unbearable, I still chose the shade with this heavy costume though. I start with my routine to twirl my sign and I get a crowd that gathers to watch. I wish we would have brought music, but that might have been too much.

I'm glad we are outside when Kyle finds us. I'm surprised it took her this long; especially with the crowd that's watching us. I hear her before I see her. It's that high pitched squealing voice that I hate more than anything, that pierces my ear drums. She might run around like a tomboy and follow us around, but she is all girl.

I wave to Kyle as she struggles against Joey. Luckily he knows her well, he has her around the waist and her feet are completely off the ground. Otherwise I'm sure she would have charged me by now. I watch her punching Joey, he doesn't even wince. I see him leaning forward and talking to her but whatever he's saying is only inflaming her temper.

I wave one last time to her and wave the sign for her again. She's shaking her head and beating on Joey. She watches as I give the sign a last spin before turning it to the opposite side. She doesn't take long to read it and I thought she would be happy with it.

The other side of the sign says,

My sister

Kyle

is SpECiaL

7

If There's a Chance

I watch her stop fighting and Joey releases her. I thought she would find this funny but instead she gestures to me with a single finger moving in a circle. I know what she means; she started doing that to tell me it comes around. This is too good, she doesn't have a chance. She doesn't say anything else; she goes back into the building. I have no idea what's wrong with her now but we all know not to mention its PMS to her. She goes crazy if we say that to her.

We stay for the afternoon. There's not much point to driving home and coming back, besides this is too much fun.

We have a lot of people that walk by and take pictures of us. Some get their picture taken with us. Today was also some ladies birthday and they asked me to deliver balloons to her. I didn't expect to go into the office in this suit but why not. I'm even doing a walkthrough of the intern department.

I see Kyle walking down the hallway reading from some papers. She isn't watching where she's going and it is too easy to sneak up on her. She only looks up when she hears people laughing. I really want to throw her over my shoulder and carry her around but she does have to work here.

She faces me and just stares at me, "You shouldn't be here."

I have to move in closer so she can hear me, "I just delivered some balloons upstairs. I was only stopping to say hi."

I was hoping she would admit defeat but I'm not sure she knows how to do that. "Of course if you need anything heavy moved or other interns are giving you a hard time."

She reaches out to push at my shoulder. I take the chance to grab at her wrist and pull her in for a hug. She at first squeals, probably because I caught her off guard. I make some growling noises, just trying to play along with the squealing thing. She doesn't miss the chance to tell me, "I will get you for this."

8

I release her and she walks away. I follow behind her because really I have nothing else to do. After she is back to her desk I continue walking through to return to the lobby. As I step from the elevator on the first floor I decide to take a break and get some lunch.

For the rest of the afternoon Sean only records if there is a large group of people. We have spent most of our time in the lobby. The security guard we talked to earlier asked if he could hire us, he has a teenage daughter as well. We laughed it off but Sean thinks we could make some extra cash doing this. Of course, he's not the one in the suit.

Through the rest of the day we have everyone from the janitor to the CEO stop to talk to us. I'm worried about being thrown out of here by the CEO but he insists we call him Henry. He goes on to tell us, "If my son did this to his sister she would never forgive him."

Laughing off his comments, "My sister might not forgive me either but she will try to get even with me."

Sean interjects, "Knowing Kyle she will get even with all of us."

We are still laughing when his phone starts making noise and he waves to someone across the lobby. "I have an important appointment and if I take any longer my wife with not be happy." He shakes all of our hands before he leaves the building.

Joey volunteers to wear the suit for the remaining hour before Kyle will be done for the day. So we switch and he waves to people as they leave for the day.

My sister, Kyle, is the sweetest girl you will ever meet, but when she seeks vengeance look out. As we pull out of the parking lot to go home she promises all of us we should sleep with one eye open because she's coming for us.

CHAPTER 3

George

Summer is half over and I can finally say I got to sleep in every day this week. I had planned a beach trip, but it rained most of the week, so I canceled the trip. Kyle's internship ended last week and so did my time as her chauffeur. She was over the moon happy to have racked up another scholarship for school. She has been collecting scholarships like playing cards to pay for college.

I'm happy to be having breakfast at the crack of noon today. Kyle comes in from outside with a couple of her girlfriends, just as I'm getting coffee. She has had most of them here all week getting ready for cheer camp, coming up next week. They were up late last night practicing and the closer they get to camp the more squealing they do. I'm thinking rain at the beach might have been better than high school cheerleaders.

I watch Joey follow the girls in the back door. If I didn't know better I would think he was after my sister but Dean set him straight on that years ago. Since then Dean and Joey have been best friends. Joey still watches out for Kyle but it's in more of a brotherly way. That doesn't exclude him from dating her friends though. That never ends well for him, when her friends are crying she fights with Joey.

I'm desperate to escape the kitchen although I still need to eat something. I watch as the girls are preparing their lunch. "You have to eat more than salads for lunch."

I watch the horrified look on their faces, followed by a chorus of, "As, if." It's like a prepared chant and they all do it.

Over her shoulder Kyle calls to me, "Hey George, we need help with the trampoline. Do you think you and Joey could move it for us?"

I'm not even awake an hour and she has me working. "Did someone offer me up as your slave for the summer?"

I didn't know she was that close to me and I feel it when she punches me. I'm only half joking with my response, "That is not the way you ask someone to help you."

Joey is snickering across the room. I think she might ask me nicely but instead I get, "I could punch you again."

We move the trampoline for her. I'm surprised to find she has a whole party going on. She has Joey here and about seven other guys from the football team. I'm sure these guys should be practicing or at least working out but instead they're here with the cheerleaders. I confirm with Joey that he's chaperoning them. Of course he is, I also discourage him from dating Kyle's friends. He laughs and reminds me he's off to college this year.

I stop to talk to a couple of the guys. I went to school with some of their siblings and I also know them from being at our house so often. My sister might not have a date every weekend but she has an endless number of friends that are willing to hang out. A few of her friends are dating someone but when they're here they are all just friends.

Kyle starts bringing food outside and setting up the tables. She already has the grill running and they are obviously making more than salad for lunch. With all these guys they couldn't make enough salad to feed them all.

I offer to help with the grill but Kyle assures me they have it. I'm not sure when she became so independent. She's quite the hostess though, even

11

when she was younger and I had friends over she would fuss over them. They all thought she was crushing on them but she never said anything about it. I never thought she had a crush on any of them, besides she was too young to notice boys back then. Now is a whole different story.

I'm still talking when Sean walks out of the house. Lunch is ready so I stay to eat. I watch Kyle sit between a couple of the football players, it also happens to be as far from both Sean and myself as she can get. I elbow Sean and nod in the direction of Kyle. "Did you notice who's sitting with Kyle."

Disappearing half of his burger in a single bite Sean replies, "She's fine. The one on the end is dating her friend Jenny or Janey or whatever her name is. The other one has a girlfriend that goes to another school."

I didn't know all of that information but I don't pay a lot of attention to her friends either. Speaking of which one of them is sitting across from me and keeps batting her eyes at me. I talk to Joey about going out to campus next week. We have practice starting soon and this is his first year.

We all pitch in to clean up lunch. A few of the guys have to leave but the girls are all staying for the afternoon. Kyle is the cheer captain this year and she's making them all practice so they are ready for camp next week. I know cheerleading is considered a sport now but I have no idea what these girls do at camp. They all seem ready for the season to me.

I need a shower. I leave Sean and Joey out back to watch the cheerleaders. Joey was a willing volunteer, it's a tough job. I start the water for my shower and go back to get my iPod. I turn up the music and step into the shower. My foot slides and I curse my sister. She uses those oils and then it's hard to stand in the tub. I reach for the shampoo and loose my footing. I try to grab at something to hold on but it's no good. I hit the tub and everything goes black.

Sidonia Rose

If There's a Chance

CHAPTER 4

Kyle

It would be nice if my brothers would find something else to distract them today. I've been working with our cheer squad all week, we have camp next week and I want to make sure we are all ready this year. I also invited some of the football players to lunch today. I knew George would be around but I had no idea that Sean and Joey would both crash lunch today too. It's not like I can tell them to get lost, that will just make them think I'm up to something.

I heard that there is a new quarterback this year; he just transferred from another school. I went to the school this morning to talk to the coach. Fine, I went to check out the new quarterback. I hope he doesn't already have a girlfriend because I'm planning to take that spot. Jenny met him the other day and she said he is really hot.

It was a wasted trip this morning. I talked to the coach but the new quarterback wasn't there. He supposedly spends the weekends with his dad in Virginia, so he took off today. Instead I invited some of the guys over for lunch, also hoping they will tell me about the new guy.

I purposely sat as far from my brothers as possible. I want information and if any of my brothers knew what I was doing they would put a stop to me dating the new quarterback. I like our old quarterback well enough but he's a year younger than me. He did offer to be my date for all of the dances this year, he was careful to make sure I understood it wouldn't be a real date. I don't understand why everyone thinks I shouldn't be dating. I really hate my brothers sometimes.

The guys at lunch were not very helpful. I know his name now, Lance Makin. I will have to find him on Facebook tonight. I mean he's our new quarterback and I should introduce myself. The guys said he hasn't mentioned a girlfriend and they know his parents just got divorced. All good information but I was hoping for a little more. I still don't know where he lives but they did say he has his own car.

I'm daydreaming about the new quarterback until I accidently kick Naomi. "I'm so sorry, I wasn't paying attention. Are you ok?"

I guess that's a dumb question as she's holding her arm and screaming a bit. "Why did you have to kick me? I'm not a soccer ball and seriously that hurts!"

I pull her hand away to see she has a huge bruise forming. She follows me into the house to get some ice for her arm.

I can hear the shower running upstairs. I look at the time it has been a while since George went to shower and he doesn't normally take that long. I leave Naomi in the kitchen with some of the other girls and go in search of George.

At the top of the steps all I can hear is his music playing. I stand outside of the bathroom and knock. He doesn't answer me; even with the music playing I should be able to hear him. I try the handle but it's locked. I knock harder and still get no response. If he is even playing a prank on me, I will kill him. I check his room and he's not there either. I rummage through his desk drawer and find his lock pick kit.

I knock on the door again and yell to him, "I'm going to open this door if you don't answer me."

I don't think he's in there and I really think this is a trap. George is the prank king around here. I told him I would dethrone him this year and I thought my prank today would get him good.

I still owe Sean, Joey and George for their gorilla stunt. I can't believe they showed up with a gorilla costume and that stupid sign. George gave that sign to someone and they hung it by my cubicle. It was the prime location for me to look at it. All. Summer. Long.

Today I had Joey go to the store for me and get supplies for lunch. I also had him get me petroleum jelly, lots of it. He wouldn't give it to me until I told him what it was for, I lied. I told him it keeps us from chaffing at camp; it would do that if we had that problem. The truth is I needed it for the bathtub. I spent close to an hour waxing the tub this morning and there is no way George could have known I did it. He was still asleep, so this has to work.

Still no answer, I pick the lock on the door. As I open the door the steam is over powering. I'm hesitant but only because I know George is about to jump out at me, "George? Are you in here?"

I turn off his music and all I can hear is the shower running. I pull the curtain and find blood. Then I find George, unconscious.

Screaming only gets him groaning. His head rolls and I see a large gash on the side of his head. I run from the bathroom and call for an ambulance. They are asking too many questions and I can't answer them. Between tears I turn off the water and place towels over George. He's sprawled out on the bottom of the tub and well he's my brother. I don't need to see that.

Everything starts happening fast. Sean and Joey are both in the bathroom with me. Joey takes the phone and then I have to answer Sean's questions. George is awake but unable to get up from the tub. He's at least holding a towel on his head to try and stop the bleeding.

I admit to Sean that I did something to tub, but it was only supposed to be a prank. My brothers might disagree with me and we fight all the time, but I would never hurt them on purpose. They have never hit me before, today though Sean comes close to punching me and I know it.

I'm sent to get George clothes. I can't find his favorite shirt and I know he will want it. At least I hope it will make him less angry with me. I finally give up and take a black shirt from his drawer. He likes black shirts.

Down the hall I can hear the paramedics in the bathroom. Luckily they sent a couple of guys and they should be able to get him up. As I reach the bathroom George is lifted onto a stretcher in the hallway. He still has the towels on top of him. I try to listen as they tell Sean where he is being taken. Sean just stares at me and I know I'm in so much trouble.

I have to send everyone home downstairs; some of them have already left. I'm locking the back door when Sean finds me. He grabs me by the arm and drags me through the house, "I can't believe you did this!"

"I didn't mean for this happen." He's not letting go of me, "Sean, you're hurting my arm."

He stops at his car and faces me. "You do realize he at least has a concussion, right?" I want to say something but he leans in to yell in my face instead, "For a prank! A prank!"

He's right. I wipe at the tears streaming down my face. I know this is my fault; he doesn't have to rub it in. "But, I just…"

"Sean! Back off."

Joey pulls Sean away from me and he puts an arm around me. I fall into him and just cry. I can't believe that George got hurt and it's my fault entirely. Joey lets me sit in the backseat and he sits up front with Sean. My mother is already on her way to the hospital.

I didn't even hear the phone ring but Joey is handing it to me. "Your father is on the phone and wants to talk to you Kyle."

I know this isn't going to be good. He just told us last week to stop the pranks but then he helped George with a prank over the weekend. My voice is shaky when I answer him, "I'm sorry, Daddy. I didn't know he would get hurt like this."

I say nothing else. My father is obviously driving because I can hear the traffic. He tells me how irresponsible I am before he explains in detail how I will spend the rest of the summer. I only nod, he can't see me but it doesn't matter. I don't have to agree with him, I know what he's telling me is what is going to happen.

He stops talking for a few seconds and finally I hear, "I'm at the hospital. We will talk about this at home."

That is French for, you will listen to me when we get home.

CHAPTER 5

Kyle

I've been sitting by myself in the waiting room for close to two hours. I saw both of my parents when we first got here. Mom gave me a hug but dad wouldn't even look at me. Mom took the bag I brought; it has George's clothes in it. They have been in the back with George for quite awhile.

Joey walks into the waiting area and looks around until he finds me. I wish I would have left but I had no way out of here. He comes over and sits next to me. "Do you want to go get something to eat?"

I sniffle and shake my head. I wish I had more tissue but I've used all I could find. Now I just have a ball of snotty tissues in my hand.

"He had to get seven stitches."

I pull my feet up onto the chair so I can lean my forehead on my knees. I don't want anyone to see me start crying again. It's bad enough no one would sit close to me and they all keep staring at me. I start to cry all over again. I can't believe my brother had to get seven stitches because of me.

I feel Joey's hand rubbing my back and I ignore him. "They are just doing another CAT scan; it looks like he has a concussion."

I nod; Sean already told me probably has a concussion. My parents are going to kill me and all because I almost killed my brother.

"He asked for you, you know."

I lift my head to look at Joey. I want to see George, "Can I go back there?"

It's not Joey that answers me, "You've done enough for your brother today."

I look up at my father. He still looks really angry and there is nothing I can do about it. I lean in closer to Joey and my father's eyebrows reach for his hairline. "I really am sorry."

Dad pulls his keys from his pocket and tells me, "You will be home when I get there tonight. Don't upset your mother."

I watch him walk through the emergency room; he stops at the desk to talk to someone. After a few minutes he makes his way out the door.

Joey takes my hand and tugs me up from the chair, "Milkshakes are my treat, let's go."

I don't argue with him. I'm going to have a rough night and I will need every ounce of strength to endure the lecture from my father. He was never one to physically punish us but when he talks we all listen. Tonight is going to be no different. He is going to tell me what my punishment is and I am going to do it.

Joey and I finish our milkshakes in the cafeteria. His phone has signaled more than a few text messages. He answered a few of them but for the most part we have been sitting here quietly. I thank him for the milkshake.

We are walking back to the emergency room. We find Sean and Mom in the waiting area. Sean still looks really mad and I'm sure it's me he's mad at right now. I sit next to Mom, "How is he?"

21

She gives a little cough before answering, "They were giving him a bath and then they will let him get dressed."

I'm confused as to why he's getting a bath but Sean's voice interrupts my thoughts, "He's got petroleum jelly all over him. How much did you use?"

I look at Joey but he doesn't answer. I lie to Sean, "I don't know."

"Sean, your father will handle this." She reaches out to take my hand, "I think you kids need to stop with the pranks. We are lucky he isn't more seriously injured but next time we might not be so lucky."

I think of all the times I've gotten hurt because of their pranks. Mom used to tell the boys to leave me out of it; eventually George pulled me in too. The first prank he ever did to me was picture day in junior high. He started school earlier than me and he poured blue food coloring into my shampoo. I didn't realize what he had done until I was rinsing it. I missed picture day and they called me Smurfette for weeks. There have been other times when I've actually been injured but nothing that put me in the hospital.

I'm watching the news when I hear Sean and Joey laughing. I refocus my attention to them so I can hear what they are saying. I hear Sean tell Joey, "So she's been holding his hand all afternoon. You should have seen her cooing at him."

Sean pulls out his phone and shows it to Joey, and then they both laugh more. I move to stand in front of them and Sean hides his phone from me. He gives me a look as if asking what I want. "Who's been holding his hand?"

"Don't worry about it, you wouldn't understand." I watch Joey elbow Sean but he ignores him.

"Really Sean? You don't think I understand sex?" I watch my brother cringe when I say the big bad "s" word to him. "Please, do you not remember high school? Literally like half of every day is spent discussing sex." His face is now a nice shade of blood red.

"Kyle!" My mother hisses at me.

I turn to look at her. I don't think I could possibly get into any more trouble today, so I might as well go for broke. "What Mom? You're the one that told me about sex; remember back before I got my first period." I watch her roll her eyes, she knows I'm not afraid of the subject, just because I've never experienced it doesn't mean I'm afraid of it.

"Ew, come on. I don't want to hear about this stuff. You're my little sister." I love it when my brothers start whining. When I was younger they would torture me and make me cry. They would also hope I would whine then they would tell Mom that I wasn't allowed to play with them. I learned quickly not to let them bother me.

Someone from behind me calls our last name, Pierce. Mom, Sean and Joey can't get out of their chairs fast enough. I follow behind them and walk through the doors; I should be able to see George now is my only thought.

We all enter into a small curtained area. George is sitting on the side of the bed and a pretty nurse is helping him with his shoes. I see the way he is smiling at her and now I understand what Sean and Joey were whispering about.

A woman walks in behind me and all of the guys look at her. She is very pretty with short brown hair. She has on a white lab coat but what stands out the most is her height. She is short; I'd be surprised if she was even five feet tall. She looks around to all of us as she addresses George, "Mr Pierce, I see you have quite the fan club here."

George only nods for her; he's still watching the nurse. She starts giving him his release information. Mom takes all of the paperwork and they discuss a concussion clinic. When she is sure all of the information is understood she asks, "Is this the little sister?"

Everyone laughs except Mom. I just look around and wonder what they've said about the little sister. I know my parents aren't going to forget this and I don't need everyone talking about me too. I don't see any other choice so I go for it, "I'm the little sister." I stick my hand out to the lady in the white lab coat, "Kyle Pierce."

I think she's shocked at first but she shakes my hand, "Dr. Michaels."

The nurse helps George to stand up and I see his shirt. I didn't know that was the shirt I packed for him. I think Sean sees it at the same time, "Kyle, you have got to be kidding me."

I turn to him and I want to say I didn't do it on purpose but what's the point. They won't believe me. Besides George wears the shirt sometimes, even if Sean and Dean won't wear their shirts. I look back and read he shirt again. It simply says,

My Little Sister is AWESOME

.

CHAPTER 6

George

I had to ask her to stop talking.

Mom and Kyle brought me home last night and my sister has not stopped talking for more than two minutes. The only peace and quiet I got was when our father came home and he yelled at Kyle for a good hour. I know she didn't do this on purpose but I was still seriously injured.

The only thing that saved Kyle last night was the call from my coach. I'm going to be on the injury list for at least a few weeks, probably a month is the coach's guess. My father was worried about my scholarship for this year but coach said I wouldn't have a problem. It didn't even occur to me that my scholarship could be in jeopardy.

I don't know how many times I have to tell her I'm not mad at her. I know it was a prank and sure I was mad at first. Then she hugged me and I just couldn't be mad at her.

Kyle is still going to be miserable for the rest of summer. Other than camp next week she is grounded. I also heard Mom and Dad discussing her car. I can't believe she might lose her car over a prank. She hasn't even gotten the car yet, they were going to get it before school starts. The car is the incentive for good grades and behavior. Kyle has the best grades out of all of us; she might even get a scholarship for her grades. As for behavior, she probably has us beat there too.

"George?" I didn't hear her come back into the family room. I look and she looks sad, "It's lunchtime, can I make you something to eat?"

I can't believe its lunchtime; I run my hand across my forehead before rubbing at my eyes. "Where's Dad?"

She looks behind her before answering, "He's working in the yard. When you're ready to eat I will make lunch for everyone. I did bake cookies for you."

"Thanks, kid." She really is a great sister. I then see she has on the shirt I gave her for Christmas last year. I had someone at school make it for her, it says- I am George's bratty little sister. I chuckle at her shirt, "I could eat, but not too much."

She nods; she knows I was sick again this morning. She doesn't say anything else; she just goes back to the kitchen. I feel bad that I yelled at her earlier, I just needed her to stop talking.

My shoulder is being rubbed and I didn't realize how sore it was until now. I open my eyes to see my mom sitting next to me. I look up and see the movie I was watching is running the credits; I guess I missed the end of the movie.

"George, do you want something to eat? Kyle made lunch for everyone." Mom's voice is soothing and I just want to stay here and sleep more. I nod because I know she isn't going to let me nap here all day.

I follow her into the kitchen as the bright light assaults me. I raise my hand to cover my eyes, I'm now more grateful for Kyle closing the curtains in the family room.

"Here." In front of me Sean is handing me a pair of sunglasses. I don't respond but instead just place them on my face. They help to cut out some of the bright light. "She has lunch outside, you ok with that?"

I nod and walk out the back door. On my way I stop at the counter and take a cookie. They are still warm and although I haven't eaten yet there is no way anyone will say anything about a cookie. I see that most everyone is already at the table. Sean is following behind me while Dad, Mom, Kyle and Dean are already filling plates with food. I see that the plate in front of Kyle is still empty and she is filling a plate for someone to sit next to her. That plate would be for me, I always sit next to Kyle at the table. When she was little I would help her with her plate, I guess now it's her turn to do it for me.

I sit down next to Kyle, she smiles at me before her eyes dart to the end of the table where Dad is sitting. I listen as Dad is talking with Dean. Dean is talking about the upcoming football season. We've been lucky that all three of us are playing on the same team although Dean is the real football star among us. I'm on the team and I do all right but Dean's looking to make it his career.

I push from the table and lean back in my chair. It's hot today and the breeze feels good. I look out to the pool and consider swimming. I'm not supposed to be active until I see the doctor on Wednesday but swimming should be alright. I'm not going to compete or anything. "I'm thinking about swimming."

Kyle is quick to ask, "Do you want me to swim with you?"

She's eager to do anything for me. I know she feels guilty but it was a prank. I can't be mad; she was just getting me back. If we got mad every time someone pulled a prank around here, well everyone would be mad all the time. Mom doesn't really like our pranks but believe it or not Dad encourages us. He talks about the good old days and the pranks they would do at camp.

The first prank I ever did was the quarter prank. I think that might have been the first for all of us. Dad taught it to me, and then I taught it to Sean. Well, I had to pull it on him first. He was so careful to run the pencil around the edges of the quarter. I had trouble holding in my laughter, and then he rolled it down his face. I must have been five when I did that.

Sean throws down his fork, "I have some friends coming over this afternoon, and I don't want Kyle swimming with us."

He has had a serious axe to grind with her this week and it has only gotten worse since yesterday. I have to defend her; I know she didn't do this on purpose. "I don't think it's a big deal for her to swim with us."

"Quit defending her!" He pushes away from the table and stands, "I wish for just a day that everyone would stop defending her. You all act like she's so perfect. Look what she did!" He points to me, "What if we wouldn't have found him?"

Dad has lost his patience, "Sean, that's enough."

"No, no it isn't. I don't care. She isn't the perfect princess you all think she is."

Kyle jumps up from her seat next, "Shut-up Sean, you aren't perfect either. In fact," she stops and looks around at everyone at the table. "In fact, in fact, you Sean, you are mean. I did tell Becca not to go to the movies with you. There I admit it!"

I look from Kyle to Sean and I have no idea what's going on between them. "You should have stayed out of it!"

I'm looking at Sean when I hear something hit the table; looking back I see that Kyle has slapped her hand on the table. "I'm not staying out of it. She wouldn't talk to me for months after she went out with Dean. Can I date one of your friends? What about Matt, can I date Matt? Let's make it a double date." No one says anything; she knows Matt won't go out with her. She points at Sean, "Well? What about Scott, can I go out with Scott? What about Tyler or Zach? What about you Dean, can I date one of your friends? Maybe Joey, he would take me out."

She's on a roll today and this is only lunch. I can laugh these aren't my friends she wants to date. "Enough!" She knows not to pull this with Dad around; he's not going to let her do this. "Young lady you are not going anywhere, you are grounded. So it doesn't matter if anyone wants to date you."

She stomps her foot and gives a shriek. "This sucks! You all suck! I'm so out of here, I'm only applying to schools out of state and I can't wait to get away from all of you. Then I can date whoever the hell I want." She knocks over her chair and she steps around it. She picks it up and looks around at all of us, "You all suck! I'm going to friend all of your friends on Facebook and tell them you have lice."

She slams the door on her way into the house. I really miss school, just a house of guys and no drama. I love my sister but seriously I think she's going off the deep end.

"Sue, will you go talk to her?" Of course Dad is sending Mom. Of course Mom might be the only person Kyle isn't angry with right now. I wonder if she really knows that we have told every guy at school not to date her. "You can also tell her she won't be going out of state to school. I won't pay for it if she does."

Dad resumes eating his lunch and Mom looks around at all of us, "You boys need to give her a break. She misses having all of you here. You really should try to spend some time with her before you go back to school."

No one says anything until Mom shuts the door, it doesn't slam this time. Dean says it but we all laugh, "That was a nice PMS outburst. Thank God she has camp this week."

I'm the one that should be mad at her and yet I'm just not. Sean is sitting down and eating again, he laughs. Dad frowns. Dean just smiles.

CHAPTER 7

Kyle

I'm packing the last of my stuff as I listen to my brothers argue downstairs. George said I could come out to school with him for a few days and stay at the house. He also agreed, maybe reluctantly, that I can bring Becca and Ashley with me. I can't wait; this is going to be so much fun.

Mom and Dad left yesterday, Dad had some business trip he needed to take and he told Mom they could take a couple days on their own. I had to listen to Dad lecture me about my behavior before he left. He said if there were any shenanigans I would lose privileges. That's my dad; he really uses words like shenanigans and privileges. I've learned over the years that you don't smile when you get that talk from Dad, he finds it to be disrespectful. I'm also not to roll my eyes at him either, learned that one the hard way. I agreed to follow the rules and there will be no pranks played, whether intentional or not there are to be no pranks.

Downstairs Sean is the loudest and his voice carries upstairs, "It's our house and we don't have to allow her to stay there."

I can't hear what George is saying but I know he's on my side. I pack my computer last and take all of my bags downstairs. All eyes are on me as I set them by the door. "I promise, I'm not going to do anything."

I hold up my hand to show scouts honor to them. George looks like he's about to start laughing, Dean is rubbing his hand over his face, and Sean,

30

well he's just staring at me blankly. As if he finally snaps out it, "No! I'm not going to allow this to happen." He turns on George, "You know Mom told her to get me shampoo and she bought me lice shampoo."

I cover my mouth and smile at his antics. Dean laughs and pats Sean's shoulder as he walks behind him, "I heard you needed that stuff. She was just trying to help."

I went there, after our fight at lunch I was really mad at Sean. Mom was sent to talk to me. I know what they all think, female issues and only Mom would know how to talk to me. Whatever. The only female issue around this house is that we aren't males. Anyway, Mom tried to explain to me that I was being unreasonable and should give the guys a break. She said that George getting injured was a big scare and I need to take these things more seriously. Sometimes she doesn't get it, but then too they aren't stopping her from dating or doing any of the other fun stuff like they all did in high school. I do know that George being injured was a big scare, I was really scared too. I have been helping George and even doing some of his chores like his laundry for him. If anyone is unreasonable it's all of them, not me.

After Mom left I was still mad. I took the time to manipulate a few pictures of Sean. I was rather happy with the pictures actually; they showed Sean with lice in his hair. They were totally awesome! I also found a picture of Dean and Joey scratching their heads. I took all of those pictures and posted them on Facebook as Sean and I just so happen to ask if anyone could identify the little white things. His newsfeed blew up with people commenting. There might have been a few really ticked off girls that won't go out with him again, but whatever. It was for my cause and I still owed him and Joey for the gorilla thing. I did call us even after that.

Dad usually laughs at our pranks; he's the one that taught us half the stuff we know. If anyone can pull a prank around here, it's Dad. He didn't laugh when the boys' football coach called that night. He was getting reports about a lice outbreak on the team. I was busted. Mom had to check the hair of all the guys, including Joey. Dad really lost it on me at that point. He went on and on about scholarships in jeopardy and what about Dean's career. I get it, football is important and Dean is football. Does he know it's not the only sport? I mean cheerleading is a sport, so is soccer. Oh wait, the boys don't play those sports so they must not be as important.

Sean didn't think Dean was funny, so he pushed him. That was how the fight broke out in the foyer and they broke Mom's table. I'm probably going to get blamed for that too. I stay clear of their fights; the last one I was part of got me a dislocated shoulder and a lecture from Dad. I know I'm not a boy but that doesn't mean I should back down. It's not like they would hurt me on purpose.

Ashley arrives first. She has a serious crush on Dean and he acts like she doesn't exist. I don't think she would actually date him, not after the Becca fiasco anyway. We take our stuff out to George's car as Becca is dropped off. We just have to wait while the guys clean up their mess and we can go. I'm excited as this is the first time I get to stay in the new house. Dad said it was a good investment and all of the rooms have their own bathroom. I would love to have a room with my own bathroom. Sharing with my brothers is the worst; boys are so gross in the bathroom.

George is nice enough to give up his room for us girls. He has the biggest room and his bathroom is to die for. I already told him I'm never leaving; I can't believe he has all of this space to himself. He did complain that we had too much crap in his bathroom; he took all of his stuff and moved downstairs. I was surprised to learn there is another room on the first floor that could be an additional bedroom, it does have its own bathroom, but they are just going to use it for their weights and exercise equipment. George is using the room while we are here.

George promised to take us out for pizza tonight. He said everyone loves this place called Lita's and that their pizza is good. Becca complained that pizza is too many carbs but who cares this is a college campus. Arriving at Lita's the first thing I see is that this place is packed with football players. I know George wasn't expecting this or he would have taken us anywhere else.

"This is so great." Becca and I say the same time. Ashley is looking around, probably trying to see if Dean is here.

George groans behind us, "Maybe we should just get something to go?"

I don't even bother to answer him; I find us a table and drag Becca and Ashley along. The booth will easily seat six people and I know George won't want one of the other girls to sit with him. I push at him to slide in but he pushes me in instead. I slide across the seat and he sits next to me, sealing me off from the rest of the world. Becca and Ashley sit across from us and they have a great view of the football players.

We pass menus around the table. I flip through the menu looking to see what they have, mostly Italian food and a lot of pizza choices. George talks about their pizza all the time, "Let's just get a couple of pizzas to share."

George is busy with his phone and hasn't opened his menu. Becca and Ashley are still reading. Ashley runs her finger along the plastic coated menu, "I could do a veggie pizza. Oh, wait, let's do a white veggie pizza."

Groaning George puts away his phone, "I'll order my own pizza. Veggie was bad enough but you can't take away the sauce too." He opens and refolds his menu to look at just the page with the pizza options. "Kyle, you want to share the supreme meat only?"

I watch Ashley's face scrunch up at the thought of a meat only pizza and laugh at her. I shrug not really committing to the idea. Our waitress stops at the table and runs her fingers along the edge telling us she will be right with us.

I turn and watch George as he watches her walk away. I lean in closer to him, "You know her?"

"Huh?"

I will take that as a yes answer. "I said, is she in one of your classes?"

I get kicked from under the table and I look at Becca and Ashley trying to figure out who did it. Neither is looking at me but Becca is smiling and I know she can't be that happy looking at the menu.

George leans back in his seat and I hear his phone chime like he just got a text message. He ignores it but responds to me, "She was in one of my classes, we hung out last semester."

It has been a while since I've messed with George and this could be a golden opportunity. We agree on three pizzas before our waitress comes back to the table.

I see the waitress walk to our table; she is digging in her apron pocket shuffling things around. She's pretty; she actually looks like George's perfect girl. The only thing he would probably change is her hair is short; he's more of a long hair kind of guy. Her hair is straight and she looks like she's tall, probably my height. She definitely does not look like one of those miserable girls he was dating over the summer; she looks happy and even has a little bounce in her step. She stops and looks at George then at me, her voice is tight and she doesn't smile, "Hi, I'm Megan. Are you all ready to order or should I get you some drinks to get started?"

George hasn't stopped staring at Megan, "Hi Meg, how are you?"

She looks at me as she answers, "I'm good George, you?"

I lean over and put my hand on George's arm, "Aren't you going to introduce me?"

He knows what I'm doing and he groans instead of answering. Meg is watching me, she looks at my hand and then to George's face. I slide over further and reach my hand across him extending to Meg, "Hi Meg, it's so nice to meet you." She is hesitant but slowly takes my hand. I smile big for her and say, "George didn't say how you know each other?"

She looks flustered, she opens her mouth but nothing comes out. I glance across the table to see the girls laughing as George pushes me, "Meg, this is my little sister Kyle."

Realization hits hard and Meg has the biggest grin on her face. "I've heard about you. So your name really is Kyle?"

People are always asking me about my name. "That's me. Apparently my brother thought it was hilarious that I got a boy's name and it kind of stuck. I have been told that I'm the prettiest Kyle most people ever meet."

At first Meg isn't sure what to say, I start laughing as Becca gives me a high five, Meg laughs too. George is quick to point out, "Ignore her; as you can tell she's a bit on the shy side. We're working with her and trying to get her over it though."

I lean over and bump him as he pushes me away from him and just like that all of the tension is taken away. Meg takes our order. Before she leaves, she squeezes George's arm to tell him she will be right back.

I don't often have an opportunity to tease George about girls. He didn't date all that much in high school. At college he dates more but I never see them. He did date a couple of girls over the summer but he doesn't really bring them to the house. I did invite one of his dates over to swim but he found out and was gone all day. Meg seems to be someone he likes though or he wouldn't worry about my antics.

Becca and Ashley are talking about the guys sitting a few tables away from us. One of them has been smiling at Ashley and she is trying to discreetly point him out to Becca. I don't want to miss out, so I'm turning sideways to look as well. Becca holds up her phone and takes a picture of the guy as he waves to Ashley. We all laugh and his friends turn around to look as well.

I check on George and he's reading his phone again. I wonder who he is texting. I lean in trying to read his screen as he starts typing furiously.

"Whatcha got there?"

He moves his phone further from me. I'm not too discouraged, "Is that your date for this weekend? What was her name?" I tap my finger over my lips pretending that I'm trying to remember her name. "Hmm, what was her name? Was it, Mary? No, that doesn't sound right. Maybe it's…"

He cuts me off as Meg returns with our drinks, "Our drinks are here."

As Meg leaves, George turns to me, "Stop now or you will never come back again."

He really is uptight about this.

CHAPTER 8

George

Seeing the team physician isn't something I ever look forward to doing. This time is different though. I want to be cleared to practice and eventually play this season. This is my last year to play and I hate missing even a single practice. I know my sister didn't mean for all of this to happen, but it did. It took me a few days to figure out what happened, the medication kept me blissfully unaware.

I wanted to be mad at her but it was comical. It was the day she left for cheer camp that it finally hit me. I thought about her waxing the bathtub and then I thought about her cleaning that mess out of the tub. That was when I started laughing. I laughed all day. When Dad got home, I told him what I was laughing about and we both started laughing. He can't tell her but he said it to me, it was a damn fine prank. Well right up until they had to call an ambulance. The neighbors are still talking about it.

Her idea would have been the funniest prank ever played. She was only trying to have me covered in slimy petroleum jelly. Instead the prank went wrong and I ended up in the hospital. She had a tough summer. It started great with a scholarship win for her but ended with her losing out on getting her own car finally. She earned the car but after the hospital bills and the football coach calling, well Dad took away her car privileges. She is going to be stuck sharing a car with Mom for the foreseeable future. She says she doesn't care and knowing her, she doesn't.

If There's a Chance

I have to get out on the field with the team and give my paperwork to the coach. I'm allowed to practice today and then I can come back next week. Today is a light day for me and I'm glad because I have a date with Nurse Mary Fox tonight.

I met Nurse Mary Fox when I arrived at the hospital. She met the ambulance and took care of me all day. She was a sight to look at. The question I was asked most was if I was seeing double. I kept looking to her because if I was going to see double I wanted two of her. It never happened. I never saw double anything. I did have every test known to man run on me, or at least is seemed that way. They also had to stitch my head back together. Nurse Mary sat and held by hand while they stitched me up, I don't even remember if they gave me anything for pain at that point.

So we exchanged numbers and once I was cleared to drive again we planned to go out. I think that was four planned dates ago now. She has had to cancel because of work three times; I had to cancel the other time because of a team meeting. I thought I was exempt from the meeting as I was still on the injured list, but coach insisted on every player being there. Sean and Dean were already at school, so I had to have Kyle drive me to and from the meeting. It was nice to have her be my chauffeur for a change.

As I get out on the field I search for the coach first. He is across the field and I jog over to hand off my paperwork. As I get closer I see my sister is talking to the coach and another one of the players. He must be new as I don't recognize him.

The coach uses a single finger in a circular motion, which usually means time to run laps, but he's telling it to Kyle. "I think you owe me fifteen laps."

"I'll run with her coach." The new guy with the number twenty-seven on his jersey is a little too eager.

The coach looks him over and tells him to run the laps. There is no way I am going to let my sister run laps with the team out here. I reach the coach as she takes off waving to me. I look around and see most of the team is watching her instead of what they are doing, which is warm-ups.

"Coach." I want to put a stop to this before she gets herself in trouble. "Coach, my sister might have agreed to run laps but I don't think it's a good idea. She's not a student here."

Coach takes my paperwork and nods as he looks it over. "Light day today Pierce."

The assistant coach yelling gets our attention, "You all seem to be more interested in running laps today. I'll add an extra twenty-five laps for you."

I want to point out to coach that the extra laps are probably because half of the team has been watching my sister instead of focusing. He folds up the papers and stores them with the other papers on his clipboard. He takes off his hat and wipes at the sweat on his head. "When she gets back here, get her off the field. No extra laps for you today but I want you rested and ready to go on Monday."

Waiting for Kyle to come back is taking forever. I know that girl can run faster than that and number twenty-seven better be able to run faster than his current pace. I'm stretching on my own as she nears finishing her first lap.

She picks up her pace as I jog closer to her, "Hey, there's my brother George."

He looks at me and nods his head. I will have a talk with him later, there is no way my team mate is going to take out my sister. "Hey, kid, coach said you can't be on the field."

She stops running and so does twenty-seven, "He told me that I had to do fifteen laps. I don't mind. I'm tired of listening to Ashley and Becca, besides I can use the exercise." She turns to twenty-seven, "Did I mention I'm cheer captain this year?"

"Yep, that's enough." I pick Kyle up around the waist and carry her off the field. She shrieks, which I'm sure draws more attention. "Stop it! I have an hour of practice and then we can go get some lunch."

"Sometimes you make me want to hate you George Pierce. I would expect this from Dean or Sean, but never you. Will you give him my number?" She grins at me and she better realize I will not be giving out her number.

"Stay here, stay off the field and don't do anything to draw attention." I watch her pout but it won't work. "We'll grab lunch before we head home."

"I don't want to go to your nasty pizza place again. That was the grossest pizza I've ever had. Even Kyle said it was gross unless you have the beer with it."

"Stop speaking in the third person." She did this a few years ago; she would refer to herself in third person only. She was trying to point out that we all ignored it.

Kyle shakes her head and points her finger. I turn to look, there's number twenty-seven watching her. He waves to her, "That is Kyle."

She has got to be kidding me. I stare at her unable to say anything, she waves again.

"I'll be sure to deliver a message to K-y-le." I draw out his name attempting to make fun of him. "Just for the record, Lita's is the best place in town to eat." I jog backwards putting distance between us, "You'll see next year when you are here for school."

She yells to me, "It's not happening! I'm out of state bound, you wait and see."

I wave her off and start my laps.

With practice over I'm feeling really tired. I'm going to convince Kyle, my sister, to drive us home this afternoon and I can nap in the car. Her new friend Kyle has a girlfriend, so I know she is just messing with me. I'm checking my phone for messages as I approach the girls. Nothing from Nurse Mary, so our date is still happening.

I approach the girls and I already hate her new friend Kyle. He leans in to hug her before he takes his gear with him to the locker room. A couple other guys are talking to the girls and I know it's time to go.

"Oh, hey, George." Kyle casually slides her hands into her pockets and leans against the railing.

I nod to her and the other guys start gathering their gear to follow after number twenty-seven Kyle. "Let's get lunch on our way back home."

Kyle shrugs to me and it clearly looks like the girls are not talking at this point. "Maybe we can stop for burgers? I heard about this place downtown."

I heard the other guys talking about going for burgers at the new place in town. I've wanted to try it but I want to get on the road instead. Before I can protest she continues, "The guys are all going and I wanted to say bye to Sean, Dean and Joey."

I don't have a chance and agree to burgers. "If we don't stay long, I want to get home. I'm tired and I still have my date tonight."

Ashley offers, "Becca and I will meet you there."

Kyle just nods as we leave. "You and the girls have a fight?"

"No, not really. I was just texting with this guy from school and Ashley got mad at me. It's stupid."

If There's a Chance

I heard more than enough. I get the car started and my phone signals a new message. I'm hoping it isn't from Nurse Mary, but I have a feeling it is. "My phone is in my bag, can you grab it?"

I hear a second message. Kyle reaches behind us and struggles before finding my phone. She holds it up to look at it, "Sorry, it's your nurse for tonight. She's cancelling again."

I hit my hand on the steering wheel. I really don't want to hear the comments. I take my phone from Kyle and read the messages myself.

Nurse Mary- sorry, just got called into work tonight

Nurse Mary- I'm off on Sunday & Monday

I don't even want to respond, there isn't much point. I have to be at school on Sunday, we have early practice on Monday.

"Take me to this burger place they are all talking about and I'll buy lunch." At least there's still one girl that's willing to be in public with me, even if she is my sister.

"After kicking me out of my room, it's the least you can do."

CHAPTER 9

November

4 Years Earlier

George

After weeks of rescheduling a date with Nurse Mary, we are finally going to make it work. She called last night, its last minute; I don't have much going on this weekend so I agree to attend a post Halloween party with her. She told me how crazy it was in the ER on Halloween night. I listened as she rambled on about everything from sick kids eating too much candy to a disastrous car accident.

My last class ended late today so of course that means I'm running late. We don't have a game this weekend and our coach has been pushing us hard all week at practice. We had a double work out yesterday and I was in the gym early this morning. Last week we lost to our rivals at Key College, it was a close game but we still lost.

The one stipulation for our date tonight is I have to wear a costume for this party. I didn't want to wear a lame football costume or something like that, so I asked Kyle to help me out. Luckily she still feels guilty as she is the reason I ended up in the ER with a concussion and needing stitches. She promised to stop today and get me everything I need for a costume. The only stipulations I gave her for the costume are; no make-up, nothing

43

girly, nothing to do with medical stuff, and no wigs. That leaves her a lot of room for a decent costume.

The last thing I want is for the ER Nurse to see me as a patient for our date. I would have rather just taken her out to dinner or something. That was my plan, except she really wants to attend this party. It's only a Halloween party, an after Halloween party, so how bad could it be? Besides if I attend the party with her, I'm hoping she will agree to another date.

I was slightly embarrassed in the ER telling them about falling in the bathtub. The details were vague but I said what I could remember. I remember Kyle finding me and she was upset. I was a bit confused by the whole situation. Seeing her upset like that made me want to walk out of the bathroom just to prove I was going to be ok. I wish I could have just gotten up and walked away. I'm really glad that Sean was there, he was able to calm her down and take control of the situation. If it wasn't embarrassing enough to be transported to the hospital via ambulance, they pulled me directly from the bathtub naked. I was grateful to my sister that she brought me clothes and was fussing over me. Otherwise I probably would have been released in one of those hospital gowns, which would have left my backside hanging out.

It wasn't until the next day that I found out why she was fussing so much. She told me she would get me back for my stunt with the ape suit. She was right, she got me. My sister had spent a good hour waxing the bathtub with Vaseline that morning. I never had a chance. At the hospital I was feeling stupid; I thought I just fell in the tub.

The most embarrassing moment of my life yielded me a concussion, seven stitches, and the promise of a date. The first time I saw Nurse Mary Foxx I was mesmerized. She met the ambulance and walked through the ER listening to the paramedics tell her my information. I watched as her blonde hair, which was mostly braided and pinned to her head, had just a few tendrils of a curl bouncing around her face. I reached out to tuck her hair behind her ear and I swear it was the first time she actually looked at me.

It might be a cliché but her blonde hair was wrapped around her head like a halo, I thought the girl looked more like an angel than a nurse, too bad she wasn't wearing white like the nurses used to wear. I was in the ER that day for more than five hours and she was with me most of the time. She even stayed after her shift to make sure I was discharged with the proper instructions.

I park in front of my parents' house. It doesn't look like my parents are at home. I know Kyle will be here with my costume. My kid sister has always looked up to me, and I've always looked out for her. We might pull a few pranks on each other but we are always good sports about it. I am hoping her new boyfriend isn't around while I'm home, that guy is a real piece of work. I give my sister credit though, she knew none of the guys at school would date her. So when a new guy started this year and he was a football player, well she pursued him until he asked her out. I was home a few weeks ago for homecoming and got to meet the boyfriend, Lance. I didn't like the way he treated Kyle, but Joey was quick to point out I wouldn't like the way any guy treats her.

The smell of fresh baked cookies hits me as I walk into the kitchen. I see cookies spread out on the counter and I grab a few. They are still warm and they are my favorite, chocolate chip. Between bites I call out, "Hello!"

Kyle comes bouncing into the kitchen from the family room, wearing her cheer uniform with a ponytail high on her head. She is a senior this year and loves the fact that she is the last one at home. No more big brothers watching over her, that includes Joey too. We are all away at school and expect that Kyle will join us next year, hopefully without the boyfriend.

She bounces across the kitchen and wraps her arms around me, "Hey, kid, how are you?"

She gives me a squeeze before rushing to the counter, "I'm fine. Hey, don't take all of my cookies."

I should have known they were her cookies. She is always making something and lately everything she makes is for her new boyfriend. I have to tease her, "Oh, did I take your boyfriend's cookies?"

She gives me that look telling me to back off. I'm supposed to hate any guy she dates but there is something about this guy that makes me hate him just a bit more. I laugh at her and watch as she counts the cookies. I take another cookie from the end of the counter, "Come on! These are for tonight. Everyone is coming over to watch scary movies."

I know I'm going to hate the answer to this but I have to ask, "Everyone is who again?"

She shrugs and has a sad look on her face. I know she is trying to make me feel bad but it isn't going to work. "He has to go to his dad's this weekend. He'll leave right after the game."

I laugh because I couldn't have planned this better if I tried. Her new boyfriend is consistent in running off to be at his dad's house in Virginia almost every weekend. That leaves Kyle without a date. It's also where he used to live and everyone knows he still has a lot of friends there.

I heard some talk at the homecoming game that he might have another girl back where he used to live. Dean and I confronted him and he denied that he had dated anyone from his old school. He laughed it off and tried to play it as he couldn't keep the girls away. Dean might find Kyle to be irritating but he wasn't about to let Lance talk about her that way. Dean pushed him against the wall and he looked like he was about to lose control of his bowels with Dean in his face. I'm sure that our coach should thank Kyle's boyfriend because Dean sacked the quarterback the next day four times in the same game.

I don't want to encourage her to keep dating him but I hate when she looks sad. I give her another hug and use it as an excuse to take a couple more cookies. She doesn't really care she just likes to be a brat about it anyway.

Through a mouthful of cookie I ask, "Where's the costume?"

She giggles and packs some cookies in a container, "I put it in your room. I also got out your boots and a pair of your pants. Everything should be there."

"Everything?" Hearing her say everything worries me. "I said no make-up and nothing girlie."

She rolls her eyes at me. When did my little sister grow up? "No make-up and I promise it's a guy's guys costume. Trust me," she waves her hands at me trying to shoo me out of the room, "just go put it on."

I take another cookie from her container, "Are these for me?"

She smacks at my hand, "If you save any I will pack some for you to take back to school." She points to a container on the table, "Those are for Sean though. You have to make sure he eats from that box."

I'm fairly sure she wouldn't poison him but I ask anyway, "Did you poison them?"

I see her face blush red, "I just put extra nuts in them. His favorite, walnuts." Even if I didn't know that Sean hates walnuts I would know she did something to them just for him.

"If you keep doing this crap to him he's never going to let it go Kyle." Sean can't or maybe won't move forward from her prank last summer. He has gotten her plenty of times but after her bathroom prank he took the lice thing pretty hard. "I'm not taking those cookies to Sean."

"He's the one that won't let it go. Besides, it's not like I used salt instead of sugar in them. I could have though." She wiggles her eyebrows at me

47

and I just shake my head. I turn to walk away and I hear her mumble, "Even Dad said he should get over it by now."

CHAPTER 10

George

I have no idea what this costume is supposed to be. I have my black combat boots sitting here with a pair of grey pants. This seems simple enough to me.

I also have a t-shirt with a big yellow hammer in a circle, still good with that.

Then there's a pair of long black gloves and I'm wondering if I should be working outside on some project. These are heavy duty industrial gloves that reach almost to my elbow. I put them on to examine them and it occurs to me that I could work in a kitchen with those high temp fryers. I don't know how important these are but I can wear them.

I put on exactly what Kyle has laid out for me and I check myself in the mirror. I don't look half bad, maybe even ruggedly handsome if I say so myself. I still have no idea what this costume is supposed to be.

My best guess is some type of a construction worker or a welder. I don't have a wig, no make-up, and nothing that remotely looks girly. I think my sister did great with this costume. I just don't know why there isn't a tool belt. I have a hammer on my chest but not one to carry around. Oh, maybe that would be bad for a party unless it was a toy hammer.

I enter the kitchen to find Kyle pulling more cookies from the oven.

If There's a Chance

"What do you think?" I ask holding out my hands for her to see. "What am I again?"

She turns and appears to be delighted at the sight of me in this costume, clapping her hands together quietly. I guess it looks as good as I thought. Now if Nurse Mary is as pleased, I will get that second date.

"You are Captain Hammer." She watches my expression but I have no idea who Captain Hammer is supposed to be. She adds, "From that Dr. Horrible show."

I've never heard of Dr. Horrible but since my date is with a nurse tonight, I'm guessing she will have heard of this show. "Tell me about the character, I don't think I've ever seen this show. He isn't some pathetic character right?"

She shakes her head at me, "Captain Hammer is the hero of the show." She adds in a sing song voice, "He also gets the girl."

I nod because that sounds pretty good to me. I like being the hero and I can definitely get some mileage out of this costume tonight.

I hang around with Kyle for a few minutes to find out what her plans are for the night. She tells me about the football game, I check the time thinking she is running late. She continues talking unaffected that I've looked at the clock multiple times. I ask her how she is getting to the game; she says that she has mom's van for the night.

True to her word, she hasn't complained that she didn't get her car last summer. I know she earned it just like we all did. Dad took it away saying she was irresponsible and the cost of her car had to cover the hospital bills. Repeated calls from our football coach did not help her. Mom also told me that Kyle pulled the money out of her savings to cover some of the hospital stuff when Dad kept bringing it up to her.

I watch Kyle put more cookies into a container. The fact that our father thinks she's irresponsible is almost laughable. She's preparing for a party

50

by baking cookies. The guys are having party at our house tonight and the only thing they worried about getting was a keg. Even when we were still at home and had parties, cookies were not on the menu. Back then, my parents would take Kyle with them or she would stay at a friend's house. We never let her stay for any of our parties, she was too young. I'm hoping that she stays away from parties next year at school, but I have a feeling that won't happen.

CHAPTER 11

George

Checking my phone again, I make the next left before I see the apartment complex up ahead. Nurse Mary lives close to the hospital and claims to have some crazy roommates. I find her building and park in a guest spot, as she requested I text her that I'm outside. She said she would be ready by 7:30 and I'm a few minutes early. I walk to the door and wait for her; she didn't want me to come inside. I'm not the guy that just sits in the car waiting for a date, my mother taught me better than that.

I hear the intercom for the building and recognize her voice. She tells me she will be right down; she doesn't buzz the door so I can go inside. I stand around waiting until finally someone walks to the door. They are in a full costume with a mask and I'm checking them out. It has been a few months since we met but I don't quite remember her being that large of a person. The costume pushes the door open and doesn't even look at me, as they pass me I can tell it's a guy in the costume. I watch as he walks across the parking lot to another building before meeting up with other people. I never realized there were so many post Halloween parties.

I hear the door behind me and I turn to find my date. There is no denying that this is Nurse Mary, even with her costume. Her blonde hair has been replaced with what I hope is a wig; otherwise her hair is an unfortunate color of grape soda. It's perfectly straight and longer on the left side of her head. She smiles and bats her eyelashes at me, looking closer it would appear she is wearing some sort of fake eyelashes.

I take the door, pushing it open further for her to walk outside. "Hey, George."

She walks past me and turns to look at me over her shoulder. I'm so glad I didn't let my eyes fall to look down to her costume. She has these knee length high heeled boots on and I am fantasizing about the view in back of her. She keeps walking, and luckily she turned around, and I can now watch her walk in front of me.

I didn't realize she had fishnets on under those booty shorts. I turn my head sideways; her outfit reminds me of something I've seen someone like Brittany Spears wearing. Tight black booty shorts, a bare mid drift, and top that looks more like a bra than a shirt.

She stops at the end of the walkway in front of me and watches me for a minute. I'm hoping that I don't have a big stupid grin on my face, but who could blame me. This girl was hot in scrubs but this costume which I would guess is a rock star, is even hotter.

I'm happy to see the smile on her face, and I disregard all of the pity date comments my brothers have been feeding me. I laugh it off because this is not a pity date. "Nice costume or is this what you do in your spare time?"

Her head is bobbing like she's listening to music before she says, "Did you pick that costume yourself?"

She didn't give me much time to get ready for this date. It really was a last minute call and she said no costume no date. So I'm here with a costume and now she wants to discuss it. I never thought of that, I just told Kyle to get me a costume. I don't know anything about this Dr. Awful show and I probably shouldn't point out this character gets the girl.

"Well yeah, I mean my sister picked the stuff up for me. What do you think?" I wink at her and ask, "Think you can work with this?"

She clutches her chest and laughs loud. At first I think she is exaggerating her laughter then I see the tears weep from the corner of her eyes. She reaches her hand out and touches the center of my chest, the same place as the hammer in the middle of the shirt, "Oh I think I can handle you Captain Hammer."

She does know the show, that's excellent to hear because I won't have to talk about it after all. I take her hand and guide her to the car. I hold her door and I watch her backside as she shuffles into the car. My date is hot.

As we pull out from her apartment she gives me directions to the party. I ask her some general questions about herself and all she gives are evasive answers. When we arrive at the party I know she has been working only a couple of months as a nurse and she's from PA. I want to point out that she is actually from a state with a name, because I can't figure out why people always refer to Pennsylvania as PA. That would be like me saying I'm from MD, which people would then be thinking I'm a doctor of some sort. This isn't much more than I had learned from talking to her the last few weeks on the phone.

As she exits the car I hear her say something, it almost sounds like she's singing. The only response I get is for her to laugh, "Oh sorry, sometimes I do that. I was just thinking of this song I wrote."

That's a little strange but I guess I can live with her answer. "Do you write a lot of songs?" That sounds better than asking her if she wants to be a rock star when she grows up.

She gives me a look as if to say be real before answering, "A few."

As we approach the house I can already hear the bass pumping. The closer we get the louder the music is, I suddenly realize that we are not going to be talking much at this party. I follow her up the steps and instead of knocking she goes right into the house. Looking around I would think I just walked into a frat party or maybe a high school party. There are guys playing beer pong in the front hallway, maybe it's more of a room because it is a huge space with a tile floor.

We make our way through as she says hello and hugs seven guys before she introduces me as her date. The guy she is introducing me to reaches out his hand to shake with me. I don't hold back and when he squeezes my hand to make a statement I just smile to him.

He leans into her and I hear him shout, "I see you brought the hammer with you. Let me get you a drink."

I'm pretty sure this is his house. I also don't like how he's looking at my date. He goes off in search of drinks for us. He returns a few minutes later and hands me a bottle of beer. He hands Nurse Mary a drink and she asks what it is, he yells to her again, "I got you a screwdriver. I wasn't sure you had enough tools yet."

I'm not supposed to grind my teeth but I can't help it right now. He leaves a lingering kiss on her cheek as he smiles to me. I pull her in close with one arm. We move around talking to people here and there; she introduces me to a few people but mostly she has a few random conversations.

We are outside when some girl approaches Nurse Mary and hands her a drink. The girl is dressed as a pixie and she is just tall enough to pass for a pixie. She seems highly amused when she says, "Here is your rusty nail." After handing off the drink she reaches out to me and runs her hand down my chest with a giggle.

I watch her walk away and hear Nurse Mary, "What was that? Aren't we here together?"

"I've never seen her before. Maybe you shouldn't drink that, you don't know what's in it." She turns from me and looks across to the bar and lifts her drink. The bartender was watching her and he holds up another glass as if toasting together.

I'm still nursing the same beer because I have to drive. I hear her asking me, "Aren't you ready for another drink yet?"

I shake my head, "No, I'm driving, so I have a one drink limit."

With the straw in her mouth she takes a long drink before she turns to look around. She waves to someone and leans closer to me, "I'll be right back."

CHAPTER 12

George

I've lost and found my date for the third time tonight. After I found her last time I suggested we get out of here but she was adamant that she wanted to stay a little longer. That was probably an hour ago now. My height is an advantage to me and I can look over the tops of most of the heads in the room. It's when I look outside that I see my date on stage holding a microphone.

I make my way out the back door and stop to listen to her sing. I see a lot of people watching her and dancing. She is actually pretty good even if she is singing karaoke. I could see her on stage with a band behind her; if that is something she wants to do.

I walk around and listen to some of the comments from people. Most everyone seems to know her or is talking about her like they do. I stop at the bar and get a bottle of water. I'm still amazed at the number of people they have at this party.

The pixie from earlier is standing beside me, "Having fun?"

For a small person she sure has a loud voice. I nod to her and she reaches her hand out to me, "I'm Tink."

I reach my hand to her and I don't hold in my laughter, "George. Is that your name just for tonight?"

The pixie in front of me is petite and she looks quite comfortable in her surroundings. She lets out a huff before answering me, "It's actually a nickname, this costume was just easy. Beside who else could pull off a pixie?" She looks around and leans closer to whisper yell to me, "Have you seen the people around here? They are all practically giants compared to me."

I laugh at her sarcasm. She's funny and cute as hell. We talk while my date croons out another song. I watch her on stage as she drinks from a glass and misses a line in the chorus of her song. She goes on to sing that love is a battlefield as she points to someone in the crowd. I look to see who she's pointing to and can only see it's a large crowd.

Tink beside me is asking me a question but I missed it. She must have realized I wasn't listening as she asks again, "Did you pick the costume yourself or was it the only thing they had at the costume store?"

I'm pretty sure she doesn't like my costume. I thought it wasn't so bad, "Actually it was sort of a last minute thing. I had my sister pick it up for me."

Snorting she asks, "Is this the same sister that landed you in the ER?"

I'm not sure how she knows about my sister landing me in the ER. I feel my fingers on my head and realize I'm rubbing the spot I got stitches again. I look at her but still she doesn't look familiar.

"My sister is one of kind and I definitely couldn't handle two of her." I take another drink of my water and watch as my date passes off the microphone to Wonder Woman on stage. I look back to Tink beside me, "How do you know about my ER visit?"

I'm thinking that Nurse Mary must have mentioned me to a few of her friends, so I'm feeling pretty good about this. I just don't expect to hear the answer I get, "You really were out of it that day. I was the lucky one that stitched your head back together. I thought we were going to have to sedate your sister that day."

I look at her again but I don't really remember who stitched my head. I do remember Kyle being all over the place but I thought she was just worried about retribution. I don't seem to remember this girl being there though. "Don't worry about it. I give your sister credit, she couldn't have found you a better costume."

I watch her walk off and I'm not really sure what she just meant. I get another bottle of water and go in search of my date. She is staggering off the stage, so the water will probably do her some good at this point.

I weave through the crowd in search of Nurse Mary. I find her in a group close to the stage. She seems to be arguing with another girl that is also dressed like some kind of rock star or maybe a hooker. It's hard to tell, she has a lot of make-up on and her clothes barely cover her body. The only indication that she might be dressed as a rock star is the fact that she has the same wig on as Nurse Mary.

Just as I reach the group rock star girl two leans in and kisses Nurse Mary. I stop and just stare at them. At first I think it's just one of those friendly kisses between friends, but the kiss lingers a little too long for that. As her friend pulls away from her I meet Nurse Mary's eyes and she smiles for me. I have no idea what just happened. Most guys would love to watch their date kiss another girl, but seriously that was just wrong.

I try to ignore what I just saw and still approach her. "I thought you might like some water." Her friends are all looking at me like I'm trying to poison her. It's just water and she can barely walk as it is, the last thing she needs is more alcohol. I don't want to bring more attention to the water so I tell her, "You were great up there."

She breaks into a big grin and leans into me. As she rests against me our host appears again with a drink in hand. "Alright Foxy Mary, I got you your drink."

If There's a Chance

Her hand reaches for the glass and excitedly she asks, "What's this one?"

Her rock star friend shrieks, "Looks like a wallbanger to me!"

I get the tool references. They are just getting old.

The host again, I think she told me his name but I couldn't even guess at this point, is handing her something. "Here, thought I would hand this over to you."

He gives her a black rectangular object; it almost looks like a remote for something. She shrieks in laughter and finishes her drink in two swallows. Passing off the glass, "I love it! Maybe we can load up the song and sing it?"

She's looking around and I have no idea what she's doing. She turns over the object in her hand and I see it is in fact a remote. I have no idea why she wants to sing about a remote.

I put my hand around her forearm to get her attention, "Maybe we should get out of here."

Without a reply she points the remote at me and starts pressing buttons. I quickly let go of her arm and I'm just watching her. She yells just as the music stops, "It's not doing anything!"

I have no idea what the remote is supposed to do but an educated guess is telling me it stopped the music. I step closer to her while she is furiously pressing more buttons. Rock star girl two takes the remote from her and looks at me, "I got this. She won't need a ride home."

It seems I was just dismissed from my date by a third party. If I hadn't seen the kiss earlier I would think they were just friends. Interrupting my thoughts Nurse Mary tells me, "Sorry, George. I was fighting with Tessa and she didn't think I could get a date."

My brothers ribbing me for weeks about a pity date is starting to seem likely at this point. "You invited me here with you…"

She interrupts me, "I did, and we are just going to stay here tonight. You should call me some time and we can do something."

She turns to walk away but stops, "Oh and George don't be such a tool!" She bends forward slapping her hand on her leg as she laughs. Straightening up she finishes, "I've wanted to say that all night."

I might strangle my sister if I hear one more tool joke tonight.

CHAPTER 13

Kyle

It's late as I pull Mom's van into the garage. Dad's car is here, so they made it home before me. Last week I was home long before them as they stopped at the Grubor's on their way home. Unlike them, I have a curfew even on game nights.

This was our last game of the season. It was also my last game to cheer for high school. We lost of course; we have lost more than half of our games this season. I'm not looking to cheer in college, so it doesn't really make any difference to me.

The house is quiet but I'm sure my parents are still up. I already cleared it that I would be having a group over tonight to watch movies. My curfew is midnight to be home, that doesn't exclude me from having friends over as late as I want. Most everyone's parents were at the game tonight, they all saw my parents to know we are not having a party in a house without parents.

I drop my bag on the kitchen table and walk through to the family room. Dad is watching the news; I look to the clock and realize he must have recorded it to watch when he got home. "Hey, Dad."

He sits up when he hears my voice and I sit on the couch beside him. "Tough loss at the game tonight."

"Eh." I shrug my shoulders. "It didn't really matter, it was the last game whether we won or lost."

Dad has the news muted and he's still watching it as the commentary scrolls across the bottom of the screen. "That's a tough loss for Lance with the team only getting a single field goal tonight."

Kicking off my shoes, "I didn't even talk to Lance after the game. I'm glad he will be gone all weekend but he will still be in a crappy mood at school on Monday."

"I saw you talking to the Stein boy after the game."

I sigh; this is starting to sound like an interrogation. "His name is Ray and I was just congratulating him. He's the kicker for the team."

Dad nods but doesn't respond. He turns the sound back on and listens to the weather forecast. As they go into the seven day forecast I ask, "Have you heard from George tonight?"

He's still watching the weather, or more like waiting for the sports highlights to play. "He went out with that nurse tonight from the ER I think."

I guess that means George hasn't been here. Maybe his date is going well for him. "Did you see the costume I got for him?"

Dad seems surprised by my question, "Why would he need a costume? Did they go to a party or something?"

I sit forward on the couch; I can't wait to tell Dad about this costume. "She told him it was a post Halloween party and if he didn't show up in a costume the date was off." I watch Dad shake his head; George is probably going to hear about this from Dad. The only thing about Halloween that Dad really likes is the tricks, he's not so much a treat kind of guy.

"So George had me get a costume for him. I was going to give him one of those Captain Hammer shirts for Christmas; instead I got him the stuff to be Captain Hammer for Halloween. Isn't that funny?"

The sports highlights are forgotten as Dad starts laughing. Mom must have heard us down here and she comes in to sit in the chair across from us. "What's so funny?"

Between laughing he asks her, "Did you know about this post Halloween party?"

Mom shakes her head at us and I laugh along with Dad. "I know that George asked Kyle to get him a costume."

Dad tells her, "She did, she dressed him up as a tool."

Mom doesn't have any idea what we are talking about. "So like a screwdriver or a wrench?"

I couldn't have planned this better if I tried. As Mom says the word wrench, George walks into the room. If he's home this early, I would guess his date did not go that well.

"Seriously, more tool jokes?"

George leans in to hug Mom as Dad and I laugh at him. I don't have a chance to say anything before Dad says, "Was there a wrench in your plans tonight?"

George throws his gloves at me; one hits me in the chest while the other falls on the floor in front of me. I pick up the gloves and pull them on. These are huge on my hands. I make a fist and pound it into my other hand, "You remember this one Mom. Remember the song about laundry day?"

Mom looks like she's trying to remember what I'm talking about. Beside me Dad sings, "See you there."

Mom suddenly remembers the song and a big grin crosses her face, "Oh, Ian. Isn't that the one with that nice looking guy from the cop show on Monday night? Oh, what is it called?"

I wait expecting she is going to remember the name of her favorite show from last season. We haven't watched any of the new episodes, we have a few recorded on the DVR. Mom is snapping her fingers trying to remember the name of the show. I bob my head listening to Dad humming the laundry song, funny he didn't sing about under things out loud.

George is watching all of us like we have lost our minds. He finally asks, "The one with the writer and the cop?"

"That's the one!" It's so funny to hear my parents liking the same shows my friends and I love to watch. Mom adds, "The writer, that's the one, he was Captain Hammer."

George has a look of disgust on his face. "What?"

Mom still ignores George, "Wasn't that a musical or something?"

Dad finishes humming his song in time to respond, "Just a sing along blog, dear. It was not a musical."

"Wait, it was a musical? As in all songs?" He's looking at me expecting his answer. I nod.

I didn't think it was a big deal. Sure it was a total cult following but it was good. The costumes were easy and lots of people use them for Halloween. I didn't know he never watched it, I mean we used to all sing the songs. Maybe he was already away at school when we were singing those songs.

I wipe some spit from my face, "Say it, don't spray it there buddy!"

I jump up from the couch and move quickly as George stalks in my direction. "George!" He's not listening to me.

If There's a Chance

"You dressed me up as a singing tool for Halloween?"

Dad's not really helping me, "You left yourself open to this one George and she got you."

I'm in the kitchen circling the table, "Technically I didn't dress you, you did that."

He isn't amused. He looks around and finds a dish of candy on the counter. He picks up a handful and starts to throw it at me a piece at a time. I raise my hands over my head and get pelted in the arm. "OW!"

"You dressed me as a singing tool for my date." He throws another piece of candy at me, hitting me in the shoulder. "You knew people would make fun of this costume."

I'm laughing and trying to move around the table so he doesn't get his hands on me. "I didn't know." He hits me with another piece of candy, "Ok, maybe I thought they would."

I get two more pieces of candy thrown at me, "You pranked me."

I point a finger at him, "No, no, no, this was not a prank. I was doing you a favor."

A piece of candy hits my neck, "This was not a favor but I do owe you."

Mom walks to the sink and gets a glass of water. "One of you better pick up all of that candy."

"He will."

"She will."

Mom had barely finished telling us to pick up the candy when we spit out the same answer in reverse. I'm doing probably my third lap of the table and now I have to dodge candy flying at me and on the floor.

"I'm not the one throwing candy." I give him a fake smile. "I don't think we are allowed to throw things in the house though."

Mom sets her water glass on the counter. "Kyle, are you still having your friends over tonight for movies?"

I look at the clock to check the time. I thought some of them would have already gotten here. Actually I should have already showered.

Looking at the clock gives George the upper hand. He easily grabs me and throws me over his shoulder. I shriek knowing that he is about to torture me. A swift pat on my backside, "Stop it."

He carries me back into the family room and dumps me on the floor. He follows me down and starts tickling me. "Admit that you pranked me."

I hate to be tickled. Of all of us, I'm the most ticklish. Add to that I'm also the weakest, and the only girl. The boys know they can pin me to tickle me without too much of a fight."Stop! Stop!"

I get a hand loose and slap at him. He struggles for a minute and gets both of my hands in one of his, and then he starts to tickle my leg. "Admit it and maybe I will let you go."

"Dad!"

Dad turns up the news again. He must have gone back to see the sports highlights. Sometimes they show high school games on Friday night, he always watches to see if our school is featured. Of course with our abysmal season we haven't had many features, the other teams were more the feature.

The sports highlight must have gone to a commercial as the TV gets quiet. "Careful with her George."

George laughs and says, "She's only hurting herself, I'm just holding her hands."

I continue to struggle; I've never learned to surrender. "Dad, did Kyle tell you she made cookies?"

I know where he is going and I am going to take him down if he tells. "Don't George," he tickles me harder and I can't stop myself from rolling side to side trying to get away from his fingers.

"So she asked me take a box of cookies to Sean specifically." I start kicking with my legs and he moves over to sit across my thighs.

I know Dad can hear him, its Dad's response that I don't expect. "Sean is just being stubborn. She has tried to mend fences with him."

"Is that what you're doing Kyle? Mending fences?" He stops tickling me and I laugh for a few more minutes trying to get myself under control. I hear the doorbell ring and I hope Mom is answering the door.

I hear voices in the hallway its Dad's question that has my focus, "It's not as if she would poison him. He might be a bad sport but he's still her brother."

George gives me that look telling me to admit what I did. I shake my head. He takes one hand and holds is above my middle flexing his fingers. "Don't, please don't. No more. No more."

I'm actually exhausted from the exertion of laughing. I turn my head to the side and see that we have quite an audience now with many of my friends laughing at me. It's not that unusual for my brothers to torture me and my friends all kind of ignore my brothers. Well a few of them drool over my brothers but they ignore everything else.

"Are you here all weekend George?" He shrugs his response to me. "I will get you for this."

He leans in closer to me, "Tell Dad about the cookies and I will let you go."

I see Dad standing over George, "Let her go, she has friends here."

It's enough of a distraction and I'm able to topple him over. He lands on his side and I work fast to untangle myself. I roll away expecting to escape. I adjust my shirt and get up off of the floor.

Before I can get away, Dad puts an arm around both of our shoulders and pulls us in closer. "I've wanted to talk to both of you. Your mother and I discussed it and this needs to become one of our prank rules."

Holding my breath I listen to Dad tell us how worried they have been. Sometimes even the best laid plans go awry but none of us would ever intentionally hurt anyone. Dad concludes with, "So if there is a chance of an ER visit, maybe you should find a different prank. That is not to say you shouldn't still express yourselves but your mom shouldn't have to worry like this."

He's right, of course he's right. Mom tried to ban all pranks a few years ago but Dad wouldn't hear of it. Instead he started giving us prank rules. He doesn't give us many but we know to follow them. Someday we can look back on this and laugh but for now it's still a little to fresh in our minds.

All of the food has been set up in the kitchen. I invite George to hang out with us and he agrees, he even offers to get the movies set up for us. It's late and everyone is hungry, we've finished off three large pizzas already and a container of cookies. I know George was making fun of me for making cookies, but everyone loves them so I do it.

I settle in to watch the movie. Everyone is sprawled out across the family room. A few couples are cuddling together but for the most part everyone is just hanging out. I sit next to George and he's eating another slice of pizza. "So much better than that crappy pizza you fed me at school."

He elbows me and I exaggerate being pushed. "You'll see, you will love Lita's next year."

I drink some of my soda and frown, "I'm not going to school with all of you. I really want to go out of state. I have enough money to do it. Besides, you won't even be there next year."

George leans in and wraps his arm around my waist pulling me closer. "I'm applying for grad school, so I'm planning to be there another two years. I want us to hang out and I'm hoping you'll change your mind."

I hate when he does this to me. I know he's being sincere but I also think he's working through Dad's plan and I just don't want to fall into the ranks this time around. I lean into him and steal a bite of his pizza.

I really don't want my parents to know about this. If they even suspect that I already got an acceptance letter they will accept it for me. I whisper to him, "Don't say anything, I know I got early acceptance already and I have a scholarship offer. I just really want to do my own thing."

I'm not looking at him but I can hear the joy in his voice, "That's amazing. You can stay in the dorms or at the house next year; seriously the guys will be really excited to have you there."

I snort when I hear him say the guys will be happy. "Hey, I love you kid."

I look up and smile at him, "I love you tool." At first I think he didn't hear me then I see he realizes what I just said. I push at him, "I mean I love you too."

CHAPTER 14

Present Day

Laughter, it really is the universal sign of fun and happiness. I love to hear laughter around me. I snuggle closer to Nick and laugh along with everyone else.

Sitting across from me George is the only one attempting to hold in his laughter. It's alright when it's everyone laughing at me. When it's everyone laughing at him, he tries to tone it down and play it off. It's not happening tonight.

Joey is sitting beside George and if I didn't know them, I would swear they are brothers. Both broad shouldered with the same dark brown hair. They really could be brothers, well except that their eyes are so different. George's eyes are the same brown as the rest of my big brothers. I always wished for a sister but I wouldn't trade a single one of my big brothers. Even my adopted brother Joey, I hope I always have him in my life too.

Putting his arm around George, Joey points to him and says, "The king of pity dates right here ladies and gentlemen!" He can barely get the words out between laughing so hard.

We are easily the noisiest group out tonight. The number of people sitting at our table has gone up and down over the last few hours. With George here, it's hard not to have fun, Dean stopped in during his dinner break and stories began to fly. Dean is a great story teller; he remembers details like no one I've ever met before.

Dean's stories do not often include our pranks though. Dean is a lot like Mom, she isn't in favor of pranks. I heard about the pranks Dad used to play on her before they were married and she admitted she almost called off their wedding because of them. My dad is strict, he doesn't believe in bending rules but a prank is totally different to him. He sweet talked Mom into marrying him, good thing for all of us. He did tone it down after that, well until he could start teaching us kids. She made the mistake of making him promise not to be malicious with her, she never told him not to teach the kids. He taught us well, except Dean of course.

George stands up from his chair and reaches across the table to me. I bat his hand away, I know he is going to try and tickle me. "You, you little trouble maker."

Nick pulls me in tighter to his embrace and shields me from George. "Oh it's all well and good when you tell about your great triumph of embarrassing me." I turn to my side trying to escape from George, "Then we get to the real story and you can't handle a little ribbing."

Someone's glass on the table has been knocked over and I feel cold wetness run down my pant leg.

"Ugh!" I jump up, pushing away from Nick. Backing away from the table I can see a dark blue line seep down let left leg of my jeans. Great.

I hear hands hitting the table around me, "Looks like you pissed yourself Kyle." I look up and give Jaz an evil look. He doesn't care he elbows the guy beside him, "look at her!"

This is starting to feel like my childhood all over again. My brothers and their friends making fun of me until I cry or I run home to Mom. There's no running home to Mom anymore.

"All right, all right." Nick's voice is louder than everyone as he tries to draw their attention to him and away from my pants.

Someone at the other end of the table asks the question that so many other people have asked, "Wait so that was rule three, what about the other ones?"

Nick stands up beside me and throws some money on the table, "We will have to do that another night, it's getting late."

George drops some cash on the table across from us, "Definitely another time but don't worry," he taps his head with his index finger, "I have all the stories right here. I'll be back another day to give away more dirty details."

Until then …

If There's a Chance

Acknowledgements

This is the hardest part of the book for me to write. I am so grateful every day for those around me and that includes family and friends. You all mean the world to me and I hope you all know that.

I have to thank my husband and son, you have encouraged me for years (I really do mean years) to live my dream and publish a book. I did, now I've done it again.

I'm so lucky to have an editor that has been a true friend and a sister to me for many years. Donna, you have been my friend, my matron of honor, my sister, now my editor, but through it all a true friend. Thank you, for always being there, just a phone call away.

I don't want to leave anyone out, so many people to thank. I need to thank Ebone. You are always there cheering me on and even updating Goodreads. Thanks to all of my girls over at Wicked Reads, you all brighten each and every one of my days.

To all of my readers, thank you for embracing Kyle and Nick's story so far. Thank you for your encouragement and patience. I've enjoyed getting to know all of you either via social media or for those that have come out to events to meet me in person.

A big thank you to all of the blogs that have supported me, shared my book, posted teasers or reviews or just emailed to encourage me. Thank you, thank you, thank you!

Connect with me:

For updates please contact me,

www.sidoniarose.com

Follow me on Twitter @SidoniaRoseAuth

You find me on Facebook at:

https://www.facebook.com/pages/Sidonia-Rose-Author/1424151237819902

You can find at Goodreads:

https://www.goodreads.com/author/show/7904923.Sidonia_Rose

Thank you for taking your time to purchase and read my work. I hope that you love my characters and much as I do.

If you enjoyed reading this book, please take a moment to tell a friend. You can leave a review at the retailers you purchased this from and you can also leave a review on Goodreads. Feel free to follow me on social media and share my page with others you know.

Love Shots: Love U series

By Sidonia Rose

CHAPTER 1

I can't hold the groan that escapes my lips. Hands are roaming from my hip to my breast. Lips travel up my neck leaving a scorching trail in their wake. Slowly a moist wetness follows the lips as a tongue blazes a trail of desire in me.

Fingers settle on my left nipple as it peaks to the touch. My body shudders and my breath is caught in my throat.

I run my hand north along a back, scraping skin with just the tip of one finger. I smile as I feel his body shudder at my touch.

His lips brush against mine softly. Gradually there is more urgency as he nips at my lips chewing on first my lower lip and then the upper lip. I can't hold back as desire sweeps through me. Hesitantly I allow my tongue to flutter out of my mouth and across his lips. He's kissing me with his lips. He groans and sucks my tongue into his mouth before he releases it. His lips feather mine.

His nose brushes along my cheek as his lips lower across my chin and down my throat. I can feel the heat of his breath as he makes his descent. He nibbles my throat and soothes the bites with the tip of his moist tongue.

"I have waited so long for you, sweetheart." His words sear into me as his lips lower again and nip at my breast. He grabs my hips, drawing me closer to him.

Love Shot

My eyes pop open as I follow his movements. I can feel his desire for me as it is pressing into me. He looks up as he runs his tongue over my nipple and smiles. He can see the reaction my body has to him. His smile is soon lost as he moves along my skin teasing me. Flames ignite inside me and I need to be closer to him. I pull at his head. I dig my fingers into his hair. I need him to do something more, anything more. I want this man and I want this man to want me.

A strangled cry of pleasure escapes my lips. "Ah…"

My brain is unable to focus long enough to create a syllable. I feel his lips inch into a smile as he groans. He reaches his arm under my back making my body arch and pushing my breasts into him.

His voice is ragged, "Tell me what you want. I have to hear you."

His hand joins his mouth. One is kneading my breast and the other is devouring me. He pulls at my nipple. He's flicking the hard nub with his tongue. As he drags his chin to my other breast I can feel his whiskers scrape me. My breast burns from his touch as he draws the other nipple in.

"Oh God!" I pant. I want to beg him. I want to answer his question. Something inside of me wants his pleasure to be my pleasure.

He moves back to my neck and whispers in my ear, "I like the sound of that. Definitely call me that, my love."

He runs his tongue along the edge of my ear. His breath is scorching my skin. I can't focus on anything but his lips, his tongue, and his hands.

2

"Oh, please. Please. Oh, God." His hands are everywhere and this need is uncontrollable inside of me. I can't get enough of his touch.

He's at my other ear. "Tell me what you want. I need to hear it sweetheart. Tell me."

"Please… just… oh, God." I just need him. I just want him. I can't think it or say it I just need him now. It's no longer a want it's a need. I have waited so long for him and I just need him now. He knows what I need. Only he can give this to me.

My breasts feel heavy and ache to feel his lips touching them, teasing them. His hands are cupping my breasts squeezing. The pain only causes me to want more of him. Calloused hands are searching my breasts, holding my nipples hostage to their touch. I arch into him attempting to be closer to him. Only to him. His hands push me back flat on the bed. His body is over me. His hard chest is pressed into me. His legs spread mine as he settles along my core.

His nose is running along my throat. I can feel his breath, it's coming faster now. We are hot and sticky. I can't hold still as I throw myself against his hard body again and again. I'm clutching at him my fingers yearning to feel him. I grab at his butt pulling him to me. His erection is hard as it digs into my soft, yielding body.

"Don't stop, please." I cry. He has to keep touching me. I need him to touch me. I need to touch him.

I arch into him. I run my hands up his back and hold to his shoulders. I run my fingers through his hair. I can feel the curls and waves in his hair as my fingers tangle. He rubs his head with cat like reflexes across my shoulder. He never stops kissing me.

3

Anywhere he touches he kisses. He savors me. He entices me to want more, much more.

"Show me," I gasp.

"I knew we would be good together. You have been holding out on me. You're mine. Tell me you're mine." He kisses along my neck. I feel the heat inside of me as he brushes those whiskers along my delicate skin. I'm burning and left wanting more. "I can't not have you, I have to have you. Be mine, I need you to be mine."

"Ah…"

"Say you're mine." He demands in my ear.

"Yes."

"Say it." He bites into my skin. "Tell me you're mine. I need you to be mine." He sucks the skin into his mouth. I'm leaning my head giving him more access to my neck. Anything just so he will keep going.

"Oh… yes… yours… I'm just yours." The words are wrung out of me. I'm panting barely able to take a full breath.

"I need you." He plants sweet kisses down my chest. His hands trailing behind as he runs his tongue along my skin. "You are so beautiful."

He moves back and circles my nipple with his tongue again.

"Ah." I curl my toes desire overtaking me.

"Say it, tell me you're mine." He demands.

I reach for his head again. I can't reach him. He's kissing down my stomach. I can feel those whiskers. The burn is soothing me. His kisses are wet and hot.

"Tell me. I need to hear it." He demands me to do it.

His tongue dips into my navel and circles.

"Yours. I'm yours. Please I'm just yours, just yours." I'm his. I can't belong to anyone else. There's never anyone else.

I need to feel him. I just want to beg him not to stop. I need him to...

Music . I can hear music. Oh, God. He's the one. It isn't trumpets blaring but it is music. It's always music that tells you that you have found the one. Just like in the movies. This is different though. It's not a musical score with the orchestra playing.

It's music though and it's Adam. Adam Levine is singing to me. He's telling me, 'he can't wait another minute.'

He's insistent that he can't seem to wait for me. He can't take it.

Oh, God I can't take it either. I can't wait I just need him...

~ ~

My brain unites again with my body. I struggle to move the blanket that holds me a prisoner in bed. The haze that has settled over my brain lifts as I pull myself across the bed.

I throw my hand onto the nightstand. I'm searching for the offender who is interrupting me. I resign myself to sitting up.

"Yeah." I'm out of breath and I feel wrung out. I'm panting and sweaty. I sniffle trying to control myself. I just needed another

5

minute, or an hour, I'm not really sure. I just needed him not to stop.

The voice on the other end of the phone is asking me questions. I scrub my hand down my face. My cheek is wet. Lovely, I'm wiping drool from my face and trying to concentrate on the conversation at hand.

"I'm sorry, who is this?" I can't help my annoyance. I really have no idea why they are asking about parking. They mention meals. Is this a wrong number?

Instead of a response I get a light chuckle. "I'm sorry. Have I called at a bad time? I was told you have a room to let. Is it still available?"

"A room?" Of course they would choose now to call about the room. "The room, yes it's available." I perk up realizing this call has a purpose. I'm such an idiot.

I shake my head and look around at my own room. I look back to my bed where just a moment ago I was panting and clawing. I see that it's just me on the bed alone just like when I went to bed last night. Just like every night. I can't help the sigh that escapes me.

I'm hearing something about a lucky day on the phone. I realize I should be listening to him but I'm not quite awake yet and I'm missing whatever was just happening in my dream. There's no going back now.

I thought it was my lucky day before I was interrupted. I look around my room wishing that I wasn't alone. So it's not really my lucky day after all, I am alone. It's obviously mid morning judging by the amount of sunlight in the room. I finally manage to throw off the blankets and pull my legs over the side of the bed.

He's asking something about furniture. He asks a lot of questions. "The room has a queen size bed, desk and dresser. You can add anything you like or move that into storage if that works better for you."

"Could I see the space today?" I think he's rather eager. I find this to be amusing since he has waited until the last week before school starts to find housing. Classes begin in a little more than a week now. I guess I should consider this lucky for me because this means I won't have to continue to look for another housemate.

I shake my head at myself, "Sure. Stop by and see the room. I will need references and you will have to fill out an application."

"I have some other things to do today; can I stop by in about an hour?"

Shaking my head I scratch my scalp and reply, "That will work."

I hear the phone disconnect. I groan as I drop the phone back on the bed. I look around at the scene of the crime. It was almost like he was here. Here in my bed and not just in my head. Damn. I need to find the real life version of my sexy dream man. I push those thoughts away, plenty of time for that in about eighteen months. For now I need to concentrate on getting through school. I have to remind myself that I'm alone by choice.

I pull my tank top off and toss it into the laundry basket. I add my panties along with it and head to the shower. It was a great start to my morning that was until I was interrupted. Too bad that can't count for a cardio workout for the day. I remind myself I have to work out and begin to tally my mental list of things to do today.

I set the temperature to scalding as I step into the shower. I scrub myself with my fruity soap and smile as I remember that tongue.

7

Love Shot

My skin is sensitive today and tingles as I scrub over it. Thinking about it sends a shiver through me. I close my eyes as I think of him.

I remember his kisses, his hands, his tongue, his words, his hair, and his piercing blue eyes. Those eyes were smoldering as he watched me. He smiled as he watched me. His smile made me feel things I have never felt before.

Even with the memory of those feelings and desires I have no idea who the man of my dreams is. I mean it's not like I regularly fantasize about some guy. I can't even say there is someone that I want to be with right now. Sighing, I remind myself I'm content on my own. The echo in my brain says unless he is available.

I chastise myself for my thoughts. Maybe if I repeat that mantra a few hundred times I will believe how happy I am with the status quo that is my life. It's for my own good I don't date. There is no disappointment in not dating. There are no hurt feelings and no hurtful words to speak.

Made in the USA
Middletown, DE
01 May 2015